BLACKBERRY FARM

POSTMAN JOE

Jane Pilgrim

POSTMAN JOE

This edition first published in the United Kingdom in 1999 by
Brockhampton Press
20 Bloomsbury Street
London WC1B 3QA
a member of the Hodder Headline PLC Group

Designed and Produced for Brockhampton Press by
Open Door Limited
80 High Street, Colsterworth, Lincolnshire, NG33 5JA

Illustrator: F. Stocks May
Colour separation: GA Graphics Stamford

Title: BLACKBERRY FARM, Postman Joe
ISBN: 1-84186-009-3

POSTMAN JOE

Jane Pilgrim

Illustrated by F. Stocks May

BROCKHAMPTON PRESS

Postman Joe was a bright, cheerful little robin who lived at Blackberry Farm. The farm people called him Postman Joe because he brought their letters (when there were any) and told them all the news. His real name was Joe Robin.

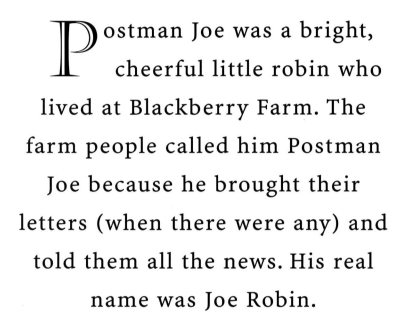

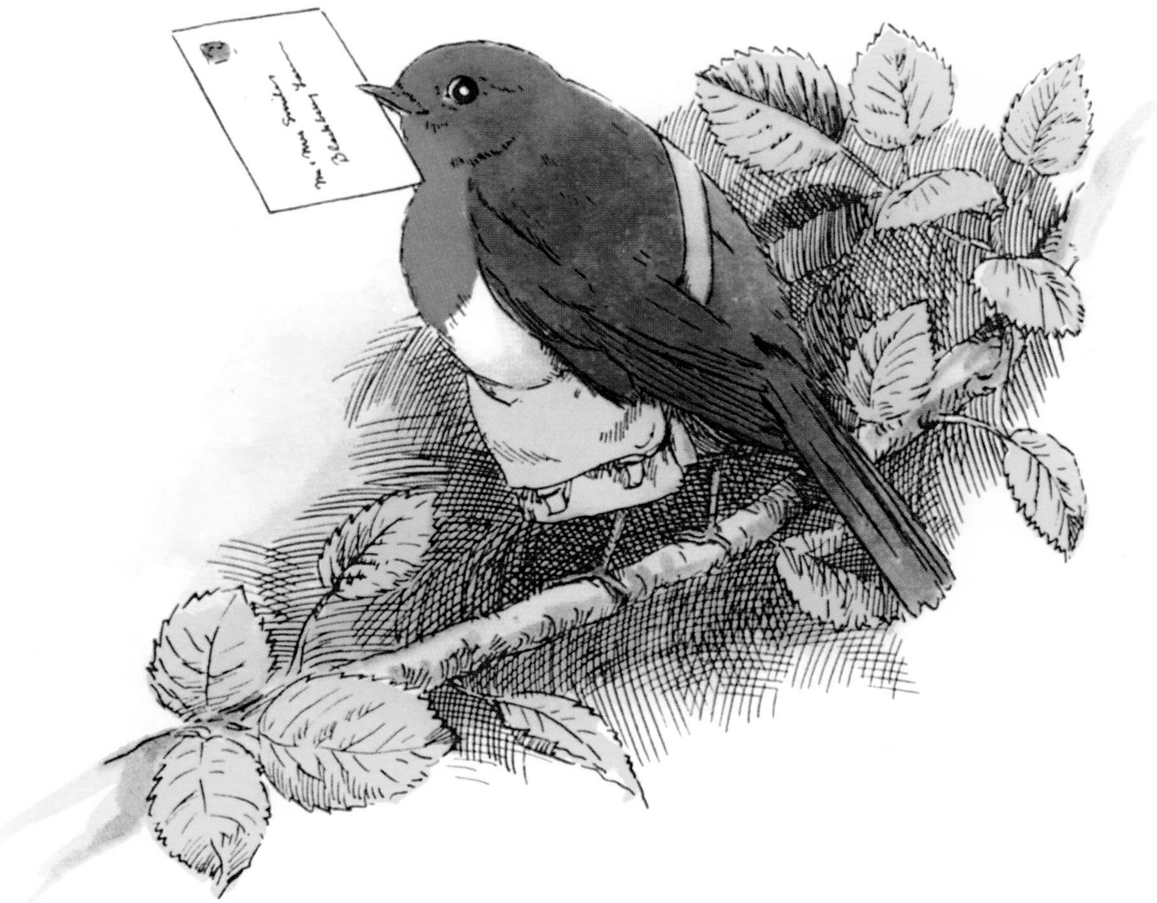

Joe Robin lived in an old kettle which someone, a long time ago, had thrown into some bushes over the wall at the bottom of the farmyard. He liked it very much, and had made it nice and cosy with bits of moss and horsehair. If he sat on the wall he could see everything that happened at the farm, and everyone knew where to find him.

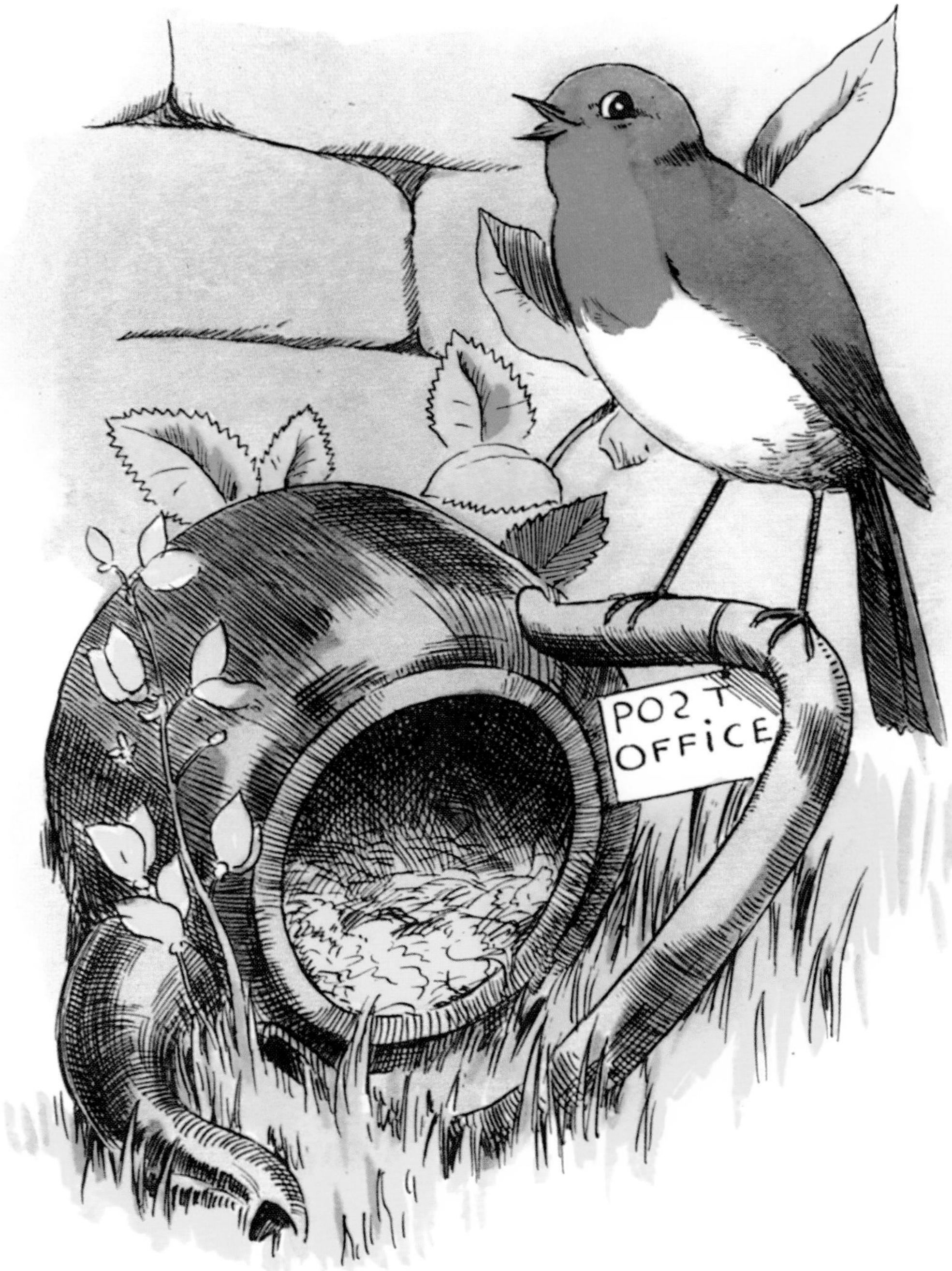
POST
OFFICE

Mrs Squirrel was very friendly
with Joe, because they both
understood about living in trees,
and Joe would often fly over to see
Mrs Squirrel and her daughter
Hazel. He would tell them where
he had seen a good crop of nuts,
and they would tell him who had
gone down the lane below the big
oak tree where they lived.

One morning Mrs Squirrel was in a great state of excitement. "You must fly up to the farm at once, Joe," she cried. "I have seen a Large Red Animal crawling up the lane, breathing out smoke. I'm sure it must be dangerous. Go and tell Mr and Mrs Smiles, and warn all the animals to stay at home today."

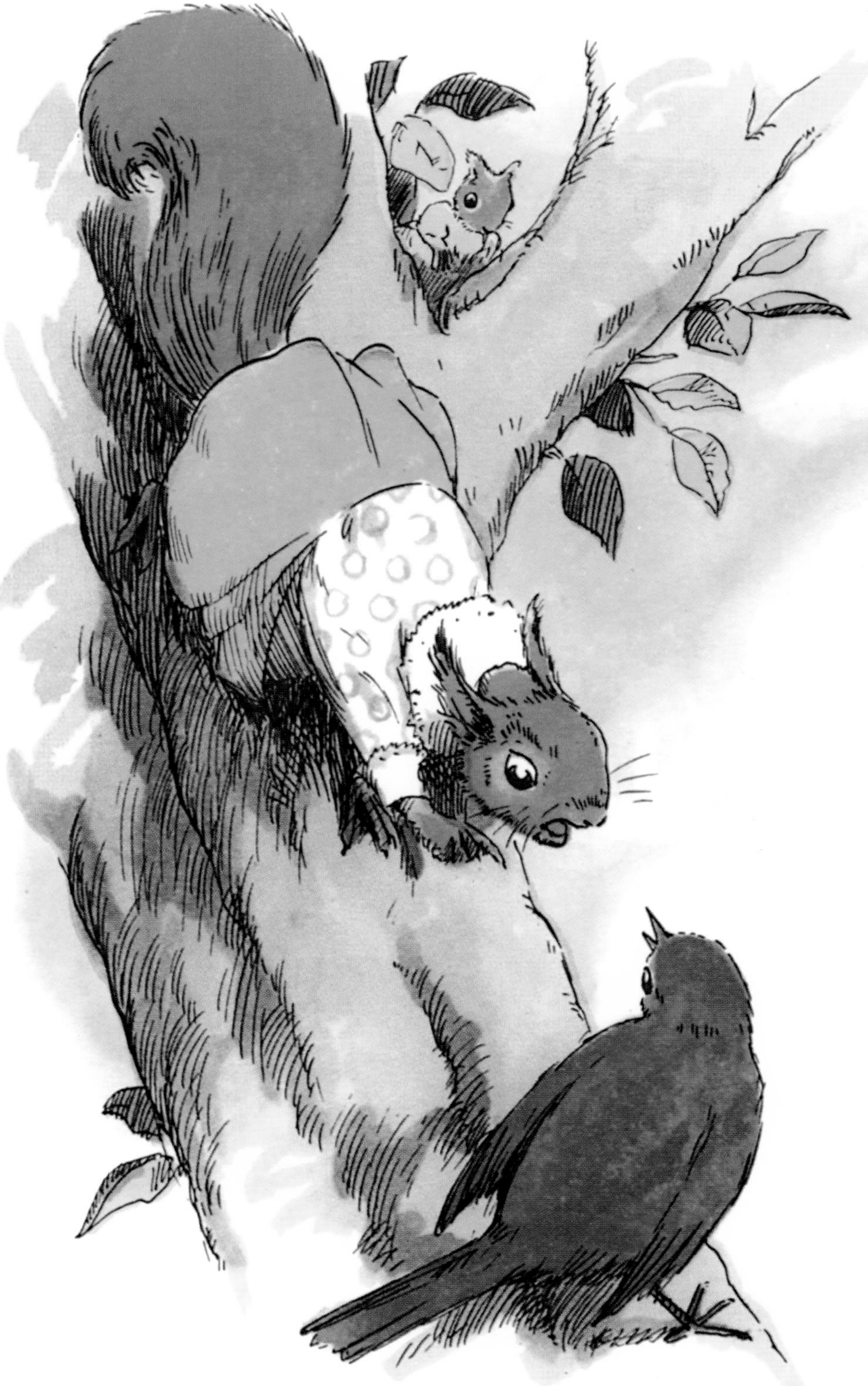

So Postman Joe flew off up to the
farm, and there in the yard was the
Large Red Animal. But it was not
breathing out smoke now, it was
standing quietly outside the farm
door. Mr Smiles, the farmer, was
standing beside it, with Mrs Smiles
and Joy and Bob (their children),
and they all looked very pleased.

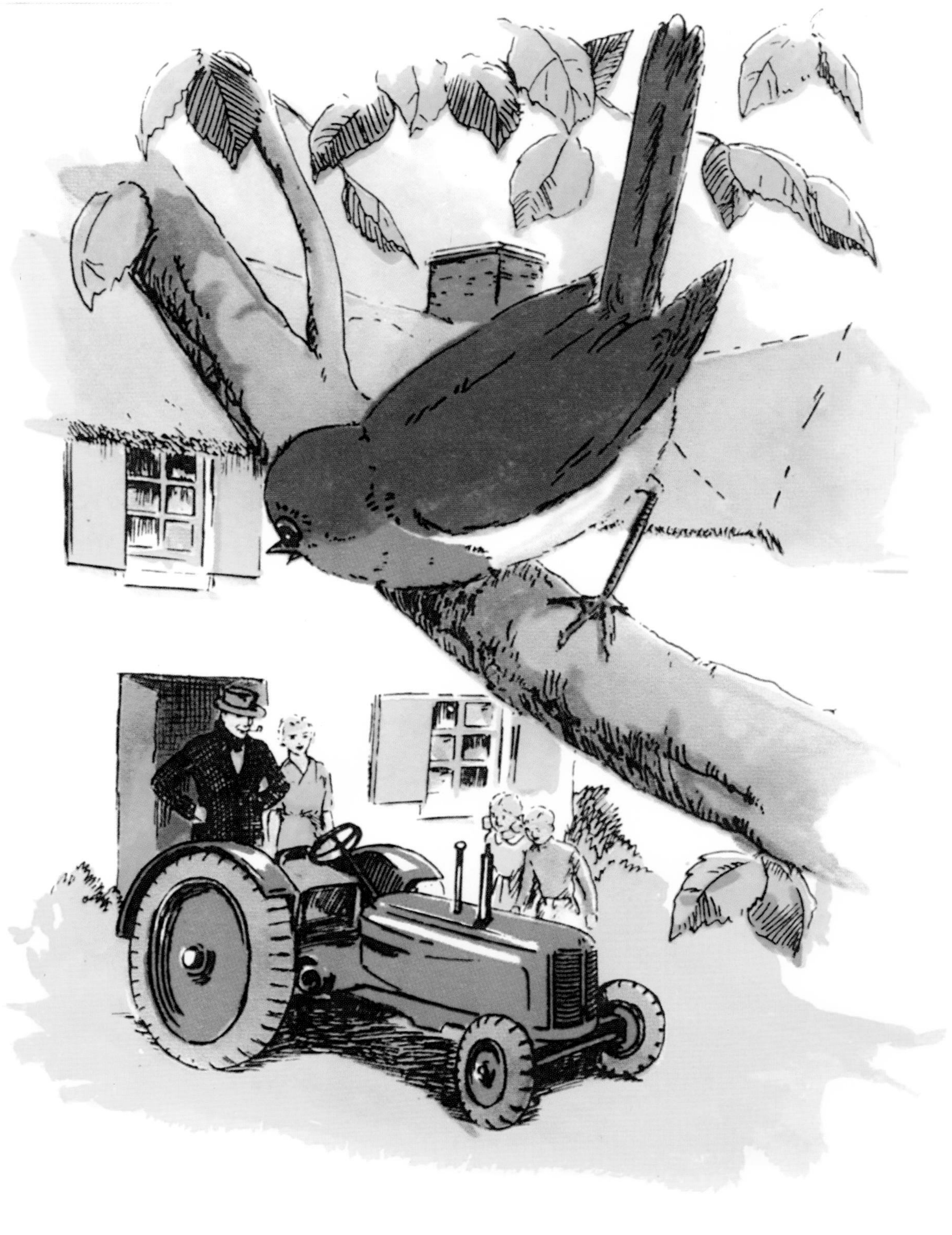

Bob saw Joe Robin flying carefully round, and he called to him: "Come and look at our new tractor, Joe. It is going to help Daddy do lots of work in the fields, and when I'm big I'm going to learn to drive it."

Joe had never seen anything like it before, and he twittered with excitement as he looked at it. "I must go and tell the others!" he called; and flew off to find Ernest Owl, who knew everything.

But Ernest Owl had never seen a tractor before, either, and he told Joe he must fly round and make sure that all the animals knew about it, so they would not be frightened. "It is your job as Postman and Newsman to tell them," he hooted. "Mrs Nibble is sure to be upset if she sees a strange Red Monster puffing into her field."

So Postman Joe went down to the field to tell Mrs Nibble first. "Don't worry, Mrs Nibble," he said. "There is nothing to be frightened about. It is only a sort of large new animal to help Mr Smiles in the fields. But we thought you ought to know before you met it. I'm going round to tell all the others."

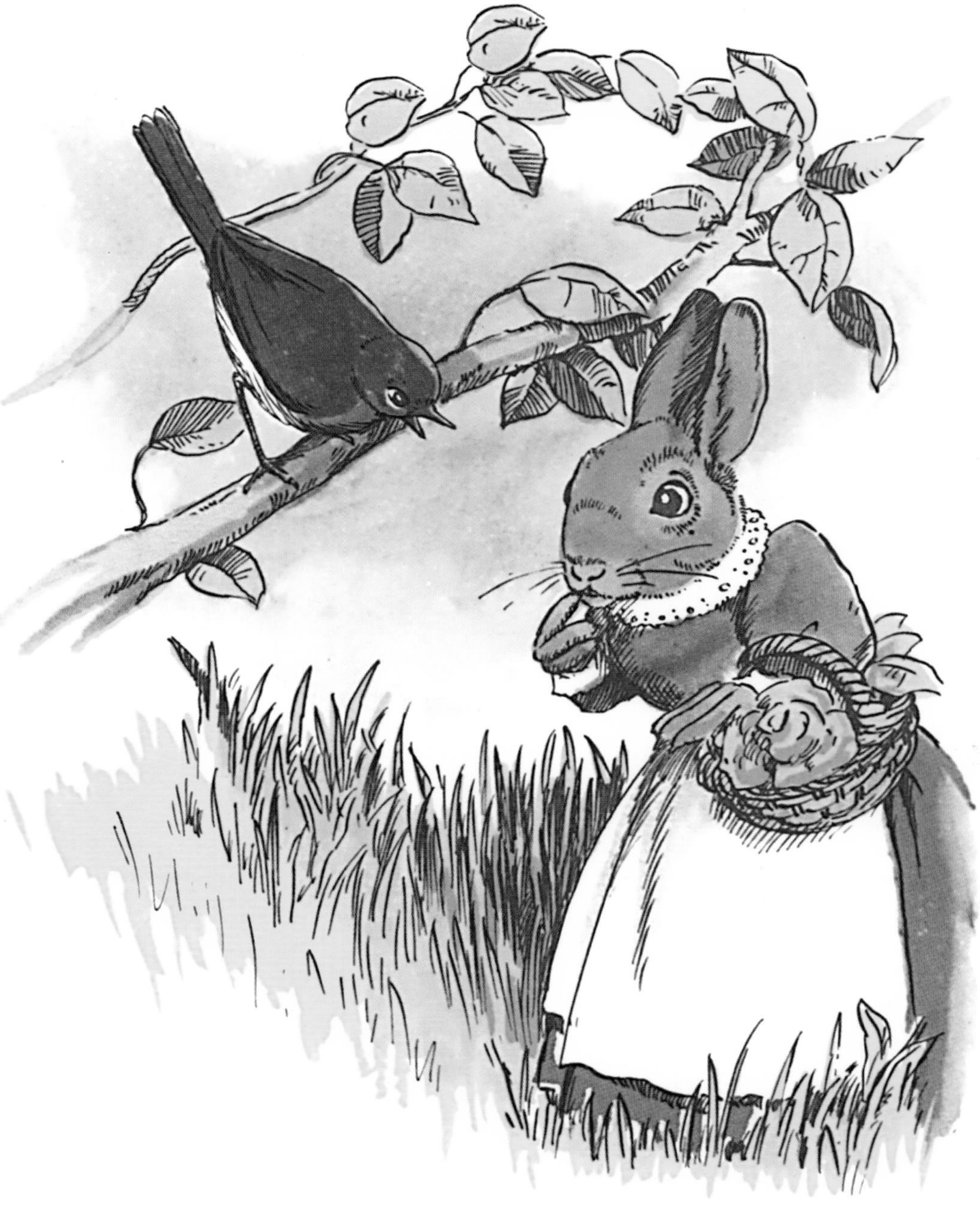

And he flew off round the farm.
All day he spent explaining about
the Large Red Animal which had
come to live at Blackberry Farm,
and everyone was very excited
and very glad that Joe Robin had
brought the news to them. "Thank
you, Joe," Henry the Pig grunted.
"I don't know what we should do
without you."

By evening Joe was tired, and he
was glad when he perched again
on the wall beside his house. It
had been a busy day, but it had
been a good one and he had
passed on his exciting news to all
the animals. That was his job, and
he had done it. Ernest Owl would
be pleased.

Ernest Owl was pleased. And he flew down late in the evening to tell him so. "You've done well, Joe Robin," he hooted. "Now we must just arrange a meeting to welcome this Large Red Animal. I have written some notes, and I want you to take them round tomorrow."

POSTMAN JOE

So next morning Joe Robin got out his postman's bag, put in Ernest Owl's notes, and flew off round the farm and the fields. Some of the animals could not read; so Joe Robin read aloud to Little Martha the Lamb, Walter Duck, and George the Kitten: "Come to the yard after tea to meet the Large Red Animal. Signed, Ernest Owl."

So after tea the animals gathered round the Large Red Animal in the yard, and Joe Robin perched bravely on its chimney (which wasn't smoking!) and Ernest Owl spoke out: "Welcome to Blackberry Farm, Large Red Animal, and thank you, Joe robin, for bringing us together and telling us all about it." And Joe Robin felt he was a very important person at Blackberry Farm. and he was very proud.

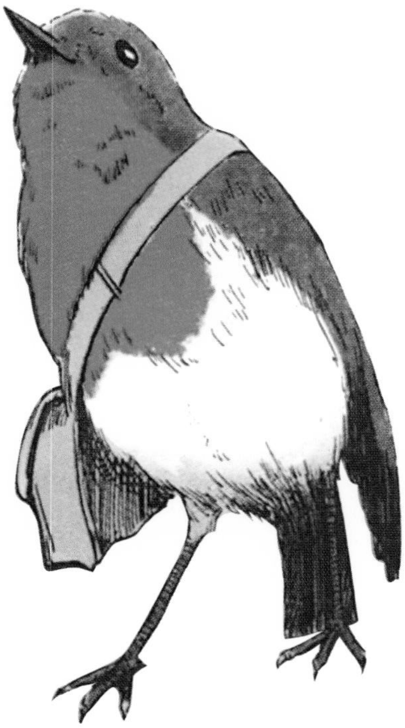